TWISTED LIBRARY
VOLUME 3

SHORT HORROR STORIES ANTHOLOGY

BRYCE NEALHAM

Copyright © Bryce Nealham.

All Right Reserved.

No part of this publication may be reproduced, distributed, or transmitted in any form or by any means, including photocopying, recording, or other electronic or mechanical methods, or by any information storage and retrieval system without the prior written permission of the publisher, except in the case of very brief quotations embodied in critical reviews and certain other noncommercial uses permitted by copyright law.

MORE BOOKS FROM THIS AUTHOR

CONTENTS

STORY 1 1
   The Wheelbarrow 1

STORY 2 15
   Emily's Ending 15

STORY 3 27
   The Hunt 27

STORY 4 37
   Falling For My Best Friend 37

STORY 5 47
   The Elevator 47

STORY 6 57
   Shells 57

STORY 7 69
   Convenience Store 69

STORY 8 79
   Omen 79

STORY 9 89
   Shower 89

STORY 1

The Wheelbarrow

A sinking feeling lingered in his gut as he made the slow walk home. It was an uphill climb, and the scorching heat of the sun made him sweat. His shirt clung to his back, wet and sticky. Still, he trudged heavily. The fifteen year old wanted the journey home to be as long as it could.

"A real man plays football," his father had declared.

He put down the whiskey bottle on the table. There was a heavy thud. It made him flinch, but he tried to compose himself. The stocky man went on, his words slurring.

"No son of mine is gonna grow up to be a wimp. You're not gonna embarrass me in front of the old boys, are you?"

"No, sir."

"That's it. You go do what you have to do."

It sounded like a motivational dialogue between father and son, but he knew that his dad didn't have a single care about school. Or him. He just didn't want to listen to his buddies brag.

He had gone on to try out for the team. But he was no football player. He was nothing like his father, rugged and muscular despite the emerging pot belly he has acquired from the constant drinking.

The boy had taken his mother's features - slender, willowy, and delicate. He had been adorable growing up and had been praised for it. But that was nothing to the old man. He was weak. A sissy.

He had done all that he could. He fell hard. Scraped his elbow badly while he was at it. But he couldn't make the team. What would his father say? He wouldn't be disappointed. No, he would be furious. He had been bad. He had disobeyed.

The fifteen year old knew the man's personality. He had grown up with it, after all. Overall, their father didn't care about them. Eat, sleep, don't make noise. He will provide and you will obey, and don't do anything that will piss him off.

And that included many, many things.

As a child, he had discovered just how bad his father could get. He had been curious about his father's model boat. Picked it up, only for it to slip off his hands and fall into the floor. It landed with a thud. Intact.

He breathed a sigh of relief and picked it up, only to look up and see the face of his father. Darkened. Silent fury burning in his eyes. He looked down to see a small flag left on the floor. Broken like a twig.

The man took a bottle and smashed it on the table. The collision happened in slow motion. First, it made contact with the table. Splinters flew off from the old table where it hit, and then the glass cracked. Crack, crack, and then it exploded.

Large pieces, small pieces, flying off everywhere. On the floor, on the table, past him and on him.

The next thing he knew he was in his mother's embrace, blood oozing from the cut on his ear where a piece of glass whizzed by. It was a miracle none of it had gone into his eye.

"See what you made me do," the older man said, his voice cold and subdued.

He wanted to scream. His neck was sticky with blood, the metallic scent making him dizzy. But nothing escaped his throat.

"Say sorry to daddy, dear. He'll understand if you apologize," his mother said in a soothing voice. She was the kindest person he knew, and he wondered why she was even with a man like him.

"S…so…rry…"

"What?"

"I'm sorry, daddy," he blubbered out, sobbing.

"Don't do that again. Now stop crying or I'll make you."

He never cried in front of dad ever again. Real men didn't shed tears, after all.

But Toby was not like him. Sweet Toby.

He was only four. A precocious child who wore his heart on his sleeve. He was noisy, energetic, and he never learned. When he was born, dad had hopes for him. But Toby was sweet, shy, and soft-hearted.

"He's even worse than you," dad muttered. He didn't even know what to make of that. Would it be fine if he took it as a compliment? At least he'd get something out of it.

Toby constantly tested their father's patience. He was loud, and he cried openly. And the worst part was that he worshiped their father. Even when he was covered in bruises he would still cling to him, snot running down his nose. The old man hated it.

He hated him. But he couldn't do anything about it right? Or could he?

He was afraid to go home. He knew dad was still angry.

"One day, I will take you away. From all of this," their mother whispered. It was their secret. But somehow dad heard. He heard and he didn't like it.

He screamed, threw things. Plates shattered and furniture flew everywhere. He had embraced his mother. To protect her. They only had to wait it out for the anger to subside.

But Toby was different. He had stepped in front of dad and screamed at the top of his lungs.

"Stop it! Stop it! You're mean, daddy! You're bad!"

"You make him shut him or I'll do it myself!"

"No, please! He's only a boy!"

"Quiet! These two brats ruined it. Ruined us! He tests me one more time and I swear, I'll deliver him there myself!"

Those words rang in his head over and over again. Would his father actually do something to Toby?

He tried to snap away from his thoughts as he reached the highest part of the slope. His house would only be a 5 minute walk away.

Then he would have to tell dad.

He surveyed the area with his eyes, looking for something to distract him. There were a few houses. Neighbors that pretended that life was happy. That nothing was wrong. Who didn't see the bruises peeking out from his arm sleeve as he pulled on it.

At his right was a dense row of blackberry bushes sitting on an empty lot. During the season the neighborhood kids would gather around to collect berries.

His mother would make pie, and his father would laugh heartily for appearances in everyone's company. Fake bliss, he knew, but it was something he looked forward to every year.

But this time there was something among the bushes. Something familiar.

It was painted yellow, now already faded. Rectangular and made of wood. Four red and blue wheels were planted into the soil. Half of it was hidden in the bushes, but he knew what it was. A wheelbarrow.

Toby's wheelbarrow.

It was his wheelbarrow, actually. One of the few things dad bought for him that he didn't really need. They were fishing. Him, mom, dad, family friends. He had felt the line tug and he pulled.

"Get it, boy! Get it!" Dad's hoarse voice shouted.

"Nah, his arms are like twigs. They'll snap before he gets anything," one of the men chortled.

He pulled hard, and somehow, like a miracle, he got it. It was a beauty. Big, too. It was a fluke, but it made that chubby guy shut up. His father beamed with pride.

"Tell you what. Tomorrow, we're gonna get you that wheelbarrow you'd been looking at and you can use it to haul in every large catch you get."

It was a symbol of his father's brief moment of pride for him. His son. Dad had etched his initials into the wood with his knife. That was how he knew it was his.

That moment was short-lived though. He never caught anything larger than a minnow after that again. And so the wheelbarrow had laid discarded in a corner of their yard, forgotten until little Toby had decided to make it his own.

Now he was looking at it.

Something about the wheelbarrow made his stomach churn. A heavy, clammy feeling engulfed him. He was sweaty, but the air around him had gone cold.

He tried to tell himself that maybe the boy had forgotten it there. They would bring it back later.

He took a few steps past it, but as he drew farther away he felt his legs become heavier, as if something was trying to drag him back to the bushes like a magnet.

Slowly, he turned back. Clouds shielded him from the sun, and it cast a shadow over the scene before him. He clenched his fists as he slowly walked back to the wheelbarrow.

It stood innocently amidst the bushes. Every step towards it felt like hours on end. He felt his throat tighten as he slowly made his way towards it.

"What's wrong? You scared?"

Dad had taunted him like that. A large spider hung in front of him.

"A small thing like that is enough to make you pee your pants? Coward, coward."

He was no coward. He wanted to say that. But nothing scared him more than his father's expectations. Even more so than the spider in front of him.

Now, he was alone. Dad wasn't there. He could do it. It was just some old, empty wheelbarrow. It was nothing.

But there was something.

His eyes widened as he saw something peeking out from the edge. It was a piece of fabric. He recognized it. Dad always used that fabric to wrap up things for storage.

And now it was right there. He took another step. Slowly, slowly, something came to view. It was a bundle. A bundle caked with something reddish brown. He inhaled sharply, it hurt his lungs.

He fell back on his bottom. His pants and his palms were covered with dirt, but he took no notice. He remembered this morning. Dad had been sharpening the axe that he used to cut wood.

"What a fine job I'll do today," he snickered to himself.

It can't be. It just can't be.

He must be seeing things. It's the heat. And the tryouts. He was tired and feeling sick, that's all. His heart pounded like a drum. It felt like it was about to pop out.

"Look at it."

He heard a voice behind him. Taunting. From the corner of his eye, he saw a pair of legs to his right.

"Why don't you look inside and see?"

His lip quivered. The voice was faint, distant. But at the same time it felt as if someone was whispering in his ear. He couldn't tell who. Male, female, he didn't know. He shivered.

"Don't you want to know?"

"I don't want to. It's not… it's not r-real. I'm just t-tired, that's all."

The voice snickered beside him. The legs were dark as shadows and rippled in a way that reminded him of a pond during the night.

"Coward, coward."

"I'm not a coward."

"You are. You don't want to know, do you?" The voice laughed. It was an otherworldly sound. The laughter rang, mixing with the chirping of crickets that sounded louder and louder by the second. His head was ringing.

"Sissy."

He hated that word. He swung his head to glare at the figure beside him. Nothing.

"See? It's because I'm sick," he told himself.

But the mocking voice lingered in his head, even when it was no longer around. His ears were still ringing.

"I'm not a coward. And I'll go look at it to prove it. I need to bring the wheelbarrow back home, anyway," he convinced himself. His heart pounded as he stood up, knees feeling weak. Like a baby deer he slowly made his way to the bundle. He couldn't tell its exact size. The bushes partially covered it. But it was big.

It was wrapped clumsily and tied up with rope. Here and there, reddish brown splotches soaked into the fabric. He swallowed.

It can't be. Don't let it be…

Slowly he lifted the cloth.

He felt bile rise up his throat as he glimpsed something from underneath. Skin. Blood. Long lashes on a wide open eye.

He ran. The vomit kept climbing up his throat but he swallowed as he ran back home. His head was swirling as the ringing reached a crescendo and he was immersed in rage he had never felt before. It reminded him of his father. He didn't know what he would do once he saw him.

"What can you do?" The voice mocked. "Sissy, sissy."

He screamed and swung the door open. His mother spun around, shocked.

"What in the world?"

"Where is he? Where is that… that…" He sputtered out the words, eyes wildly searching. Inside his head, thousands of crickets chirped to match the ringing noise. His eyes rested on the knife on the cutting board.

"Calm down, honey. Take a deep breath. What happened? Oh, you're shaking…"

"I can't- I can't. Mom, that piece of garbage. I-"

He felt mom's arms wrap around him and he froze.

"Hush. Whatever it is, it's just your emotions winning over you. Take a deep breath. I don't want you to hurt yourself."

He had something to do, but it was gonna be dangerous. For now, he let himself relax in her embrace.

"Good. Calm down. Take a seat. I'm glad you're okay. You should have seen yourself."

"Sorry…"

"Just don't do it again. You'll scare your brother."

"Huh?"

He looked up at mom, who was looking at the doorway to the other room. Toby stood there, icing smeared on his lips. He had been eating cake. Something special must have happened for mom to let him eat cake.

"I thought - He… Toby. He was there. He was bundled up, mom. And he was… dead."

"What nonsense is that?"

"Dad… he said… he said… and the axe this morning…"

He heard his mom laugh.

"I knew I shouldn't have let you try out. Did you hit your head? Why is my son going to play football and coming back with weird stories?"

"I... I'm sorry."

He lets out a sigh. The ringing in his ears was gone. Maybe she was right. He did have a bad fall earlier.

"...Cake."

"Just felt like it," mom said. "We deserve it."

"Dad will be angry."

"...Dear, you know. I've been wrong. All this time I clung to a man that used to be kind to me. But now, I know where my priorities lie. With you."

He never thought he'd hear her say that. A sense of relief washed over him. Mom loved him, but she was never on their side. She had loved him too much.

"Uh, mom?"

"Hm?"

"Where's the wheelbarrow?"

He wanted it to be over, but he just had to be sure. He had to.

"That old thing? I used it to take out some trash. It's old and broken, so I thought I'd leave it there while I'm at it."

"...Oh."

Mom smiled at him. He never realized she could smile like that. Happily.

"Come, give me another hug."

He sank his face into her bosom, breathing in the sweet scent of vanilla extract. But there was something else. A cloying, metallic smell that made him dizzy.

He turned his head and saw it. It was small. A tiny, button-sized stain on her apron. He remembered that smell, felt the scar on his ear tingle.

He looked up at mom, who smiled at him. He smiled back.

Maybe he wasn't wrong about what was in the wheelbarrow after all.

ABOUT THE AUTHOR

Lizzette Adele Ardeña

"Addie" is a freelance content writer based in the Philippines. She works on articles and short story assignments after finishing work at her primary workplace. When it comes to writing, she enjoys horror the most.

Since starting freelance writing in 2017, she has delivered short stories, eBooks, and interactive fiction scripts in various genres. Horror and thriller are her most predominant works.

In her free time, she crochets children's clothes while watching horror movies or listening to podcasts about serial killers. Addie loves potatoes and dairy products.

She currently lives with her family, including three dogs and a cat.

STORY 2
Emily's Ending

Well, here I am, alone with me and my computer, no one to bother me in my dark damp room, I'm free from the world and its annoyance.... On my wall is a poster of a beautiful movie actress Melissa... on my desk some drinks and tissue paper... and on my screen is a video of bunch of women covering themselves in chocolate and a guy with a gimp mask ready to punish them with a whip. This is what I enjoy, it's been this way for a long time and will probably always be.

I think it's a problem for me lately, my co-worker Emily has been avoiding me, she probably thinks I reek or have thoughts about her... well it's not true. But when you look into the number of things I have, it's hard to look at people without comparing it to some actress you saw on the internet tying themselves up for all sorts of sexual punishments.

I can't help it, it's who I am, always have been since the day I found out about porn. My father forbade me to look into anything nude and sexual, he'd forbid me from looking at those revealing movies on the TV.

One time, when I was a kid and watching a girls mud wrestling competition, my father noticed what I was watching and yelled "Micah! What the shit are you watching? You damned devil!", he'd then pull out his belt and beat me savagely with it. It didn't stop me from pursuing further.

One day, I merely searched up the word "sex", I just wanted to learn, that's all. I merely looked up the term on Wikipedia, and despite its professional and dull description, I was excited to learn more of it, and the internet has more to show me.

I was exposed to degeneracy. Ever heard the term "the internet is for porn"? It's true, stuff like this isn't easy to get in the real world nowadays, but what sort of stuff did I see? Well, it was "merely" just a blowjob, at first... then it escalated into threesome, into feet play, into amputation fetishes, into more and more and more. Stuff that would scar a normal person for life, but not me.

I was dragged into this world of, it's like the internet is the hook, porn is its bait and I am the cod. And every time the internet thinks the cod is getting sick of the same taste of the bait, it replaces it with something new to reel it back in.

Well that's the gist of my pathetic life story, I still am this way, and now years later living alone on this tiny cramped apartment working at retail, I seek only to pleasure myself and bury myself in a world of fantasies, I know it's wrong, really, but it just feels so right, before becoming wrong again... then wanting to feel right again. It's like a loop, but what can I say? It's not like I'm hurting people.

I know it's a cycle, but what can I say? It's not like I'm hurting people. I'd never do these sorts of things in real life... well that is until I hit a revelation. I am bored of it. I've seen a lifetime of porn and all its fetishes. I've read dozens of Hentai and followed a lot of nudity artists online. I have become so desensitized; I've no longer enjoyed it.

What do I do now? All the things I've seen are more than several generations of knowledge of explicit material... how do I get more?

Well I tried to look into... niche porn websites, they cater towards people like me, the ones that only want to fulfill their carnal desires.

But they're all so expensive, some charge a couple thousand a month, no I can't afford it... until I saw one website that said DESIRE.COM with a description that promised to please no matter what.

The site called to me, it felt like destiny; truly it must be I thought. Well I said to myself "well what's the harm?.", and so I clicked on it. And it brought me to a web page, with an extremely dull looking design. The background is just gray, and there isn't much for the eye.

It doesn't have any sort of content on the site, except words that read "AI GENERATOR THAT CAN GENERATE ANYTHING AND MORE WITH NO RESTRICTION, YOUR DESIRES FULFILLED", and a box below that asked me to enter my prompt.

Huh, I thought it was odd, it's an AI generation tool? Well I seen AI generators before, but one with absolutely no restriction? Quite unusual for an AI tool you'd expect to find, but I guess that's what makes it special.

I looked at my wall, and remembered the poster, so to test it, I simply typed for Melissa blowing a guy off in an alleyway... and it generated a video exactly in real life of Melissa doing exactly that to some random guy I don't even know about, for 4 minutes and 27 seconds.

Curious, is this a real video...? No, it says generated, so it's fake... but how does it do that? I tried verifying if it makes up a video by simply typing my name and with a prompt "Micah getting a threesome with a nun and female schoolteacher". What do you know, it showed a video of me, or at least what looks like me, having intercourse with two ladies that I just described, so it must be the real deal?

I can finally reprieve of myself an endless boredom, and I have free creative liberty to do what I want. Anything I want to do... you know, Emily is sort of cute. She's been eying me for a while now, I just know it. But I don't have the courage to speak to her, I'm not destined for any sort of companionship, but does it matter? I have her here in my fingertips.

And so, I did, I willed my desires and typed "Emily getting tied up and being spanked by a big hulky man". And it showed exactly the Emily from work! I didn't even type a last name... now that I thought of it, I never did so for my other prompts, did I? Yes, this site must be aware... now I get it, it can look into me.

I smiled; I haven't genuinely smiled in a long time. I have what I desired, everything. With bliss and thoughts of Emily, I jacked off to her being sadistically spanked by this hulking figure. Did I feel remorse? No, she's not really being hurt, it's all just generated, no one is being harmed.

So why stop? I made more compromising videos of Emily, I made her get whipped, publicly strip, and attend gang bangs... this was all so fun. I can be specific too, I can have even mythical creatures come up and be part of the video, ogres? Sure. Goblins, why not? Elves, yeah! It's all there...

But I want more, it's never enough, I decided to engross myself all night thinking of the specific things I want done to Emily... consent isn't needed when it isn't real right? All the depravities of the world shall be cursed upon her likeness and so it shall be done.

Such a wonderful sight, it's a pleasure like I've never seen before. I can do anything I want with her, amazing... anything with no consequences. Then, whenever the video ends, there's merely a dark screen afterwards before I generate another video, and all I see is my eyes and face. I can't explain it, but I don't want to look at myself, no... I need to hide my face, so I don't have to face my reality.

I donned a ski mask in my closet, perfect, my eyes can just barely be seen and my mouth only slightly visible. I feel like I've taken a guilt off my shoulders, like I'm truly me. Perfect, no guilt, the real me without burden of morality.

As I continue my decadent streak, I decided to be a bit braver... I opted for something further beyond than I was used to. I wanted to do more like Candle burning, live amputation... scarring. But as I entered my prompt, the website suddenly emitted a PING noise, admittedly I was a bit startled by it, and a text window popped up that said "YOUR AI GENERATION USAGE LIMIT HAS NOW BEEN EXCEEDED, CONTINUING WILL NOW COST YOU A FAIR EXCHANGE".

Well know, it seems like I have to pay? It never told me that before, but it didn't even give me any sort of payment options and the message closed as soon as I read it all. The website didn't seem to change... except for one thing, on top of the text box for giving the prompt, It reads Emily's Ending.

Emily's Ending... huh? Now what could that mean? It's not of any matter of course; I still have an extreme urge... I decided for Emily's ending... I wanted to see the best happy ending I could possibly want. And so, I typed in, extreme. That's it. Extreme...

And what I saw, was something beyond art, Emily was in a dark cold grey room, seemingly unresponsive and tied dangling from sharp hooks from the ceiling her body exposed bare. Although her eyes were covered, I could recognize her body and hair... speaking of her hair, a lot of it was pulled out.

And her stomach had stitches on her, and that's when I realized her organs were well kept from jars in the background. The non-essential ones like the kidney, the colon, and the stomach. all kept in a jar with a clear liquid, perfectly labeled.

I didn't feel scared, but intrigued, and I got only more intrigued when a hooded man wearing a donkey mask entered the video. The man was tall, imposing, and seemingly never makes any verbal noises and the mask was soulless, it did not cover the eyes and yet I couldn't even see his eyes, like only a void in those empty spaces.

The donkey man looked directly at me, I assume as if addressing the viewer, and nodded. I heard Emily mutter something, she whimpered a "u-uuhh", she couldn't even talk. The Donkey man then punched her hard in the gut with his bare fist, and his fist looked hard and firm, I don't even think it's organic, but I could tell what it's made off.

Emily seemed to passed out, and the donkey man pulled out a marker from his front pocket in his jacket. He opened her mouth and made a line on her tongue, then he made a dotted line on her crotch area, and he made one more circular line on her chest where heart should be.

The masked man then pullet out a scalpel, it looked like there was dry blood on it. I couldn't really figure out what is happening, I was so entranced and I couldn't look away. Just as he was slowly and gently reaching for the line on her crotch, the video suddenly cuts. It cuts to what looks like the donkey man smashing what remains of her body apart and then it cuts again, this time the donkey man is half naked and doing a dance, the video quality was getting poorer and poorer.

I'm not even aware of what's going on, I don't even know. But it was entrancing, then the video ends, and I could no longer generate any new prompts. The website then redirected me to a new page that said, "CONGRATULATIONS, THANK YOU FOR TRYING OUR EXPERIMENT, WE SHALL REWARD OUR EARLY CUSTOMER, EXPECT IT SOON!"

Well, I have no idea how I'm going to receive that when I can't provide my address. But I didn't have time to worry about that, I realized time has passed so much that I'm supposed to be working, so I took off my mask and called my boss to inform him that'd I'd be coming a bit later than usual, but when he picked up, he told me not to come, Emily was found dead.

Surprised, I looked it up on my computer, checking the latest crime reports near my area, and it was true. She was brutalized in the same manner as I saw in the video. Her organs are missing, the same organs missing in the video, now including the tongue, vagina and heart.

As soon as I tried to process what happened, I heard a doorbell. I had a shiver down my spine, reading this, it scared me. Am I next? I was afraid. But the doorbell kept ringing, at this point I decided to answer, no point in jumping to conclusions.

I decided to answer, but I was a bit paranoid, I wore the mask I wore just now before approaching the door and then looked into its eye socket. To my surprise, no one was around. I was still very scared to answer it but I braved it and opened the door. What I found was no one to greet me but a package that looked wet.

A note on the package said "CONGRATULATIONS". I closed the door to bring in the package and open it... and I was given a cut open vagina, heart and tongue. I dropped it on the floor, speechless. I didn't call the police, I don't want to be indicted.

No, I just smiled, I don't know why but I just smiled. I decided to keep the box under my bed. A souvenir of such fond memories that I can look back to. But now I'm bored... I decided to go back to the website for some fun. This time, a video was already given before I even typed in a prompt. It was the same donkey masked man... he was looking into me directly.

He nodded, and I nodded back. It seems like he knows me, and so I waved and he waved back. He understands me? I decided to take off my mask, the one I was wearing, and then as I predicted, he did it too, he took of his mask, and his face... It was me but he had no eyes, just the same empty void.

I am him, and he is me. I get it now, we are the same. He made a wide smile, and came closer to the screen, his face now covers it. I wasn't scared, but relieved. I just stared at him and he stared at me back. There is something soothing at looking at him.

I then hear a voice coming from the computer, "the way you were, always will be". I've embraced this feeling, I accepted it, this is who I am, and I enjoy it. No remorse and guilt, It is the best feeling I've ever had... and I'll never stop.

The website then refreshes. And asks me to give a prompt. This time, the name Emily is marked with a breakthrough line. And underneath it says "GENERATION LIMIT REACHED WARNING". Well, it seems like I need to provide, and so I shall... now how about Melissa?

ABOUT THE AUTHOR

Zairol Adham Bin Zainuddin

Hey there, It's me, Zairol.

I'm a guy who likes to write. Why do I like to write? Because writing is easy, look how easy it is to put words like I am doing right now. All I have to do is move my fingers on a keyboard or tablet and words come out. Simple as that.

I have studied commerce, and have taken a keen interest in the medical field, I hope one day to further myself in the field of medicine but as of right now, I'd like to gain some experience in the field of creative, content and copy-writing.

Now aside from talking about me and my dreams, what have I done previously? In terms of writing I made a complex murder story and have made a few guides here and there on certain video games. It's a lot more work than you think, but I enjoy doing it and I learnt a lot from it.

That's all there is of the current, If you want to know more about me, go ahead and message me and I'll shoot a reply. Maybe we can discuss work opportunities and we'll be able to collaborate together.

zairoladham@gmail.com

www.linkedin.com/in/zairol-adham-bin-zainuddin-6a350826b (LinkedIn)

STORY 3

The Hunt

I've always loved my annual hunting trips. I loved getting out and about, feeling the fresh air against my skin, and picking a target. The adrenaline was like nothing I had ever felt before.

This year, it's going to be even better; this year I'll have company again! Now, the people I'm going with haven't always been my favorite people, I'll admit. Jack and his friends bullied me a lot in school, but they've been making a really conscious effort to be kinder to me since Tegan died.

We've been hanging out a lot to try and fill the void, I guess. We were always in the same friend group, but we never got along as they would emotionally and physically bully me pretty severely. Tegan was the person who held us all together. When she was found murdered last year, the world just seemed to go cold, and everything changed.

Even those of us who didn't get along with each other quickly came together for familiarity and support. It was hard for me to hang out with them after what they had put me through, but I did it anyway, for Tegan.

When I mentioned my annual camping trip to Jack and the boys, they quickly asked if I wanted company. I don't know if they genuinely want to come and spend time with me or if they're scared that I too will meet the same fate that Tegan had.

Her murder has gone unsolved, you see. They've closed it as a cold case which means the murderer was still at large. This alone has everyone pretty on edge with fear that it will happen again. If my parents were around, I'm sure they would disapprove of my hunting trips greatly, but they're always off on planes in foreign countries eating caviar while I'm home alone 99% of the time.

This has caused me to become independent and pick up some new hobbies, like my annual hunting trips.

"Bianca?", Jamie, one of Jack's friends hesitantly calls from behind me. As he saw my eyes flick up to the rear-view mirror to look at him, he gulps. "Sorry, it just seemed like you were stuck in your thoughts."

He wasn't wrong. "Sorry, I was just thinking about how much I needed this trip.", I replied with a sigh.

"Shall I sing you a song then?", Caleb says sarcastically.

"Please, no." I reply rolling my eyes and laughing.

Within three seconds, Jamie, Jack, Caleb, and Sebastian began busting out their very own, very awful rendition of Piano Man by Billy Joel. It's hard to believe that these are the same people that bullied me for so many years.

"Please, enough, I can't handle this. You'll put me off my hunting game." I jokingly say to them as I turn my own music up in the front.

"Oh gosh, we wouldn't want to do that, would we?" Sebastian says sarcastically.

The rest of the drive was filled with stupid, sexist hunting jokes, arguments about who can hunt the best, and the question 'are we there yet?' being asked far too many times.

Finally, we pull down a pine-needle-covered track. The boys in the back quickly shut up as they see where I have brought them.

"Bianca", Jack swallowed nervously. "This is the last place Tegan was seen alive."

I stay quiet and drive along as they all look at each other in the back with nervous faces as if they'd seen a ghost.

I stop the car and Caleb speaks up. "Bianca, why are we here, of all places?"

"Tegan and I used to go camping and hunting here." I started, staring off into the distance. "She's actually the one that taught me how to hunt a few years ago. She and I used to come here every year. Last year, I came alone because we had argued weeks before and she cancelled, but it didn't feel the same. I just miss her I guess, so I keep coming back."

I looked around at them and noticed all of their faces had softened in sympathy, except for Sebastian's.

"Were you here when she went missing?" he asked bitterly.

"Sebastian!" Jack and Jamie yell at the same time.

"Isn't it a fair question?" He says again.

See, Sebastian had been dating Tegan for many years. Whenever he got even a sniff of a trail he could follow, he suddenly turned into an FBI agent. I get it, he loved her, but the local police did the best they could with the resources they had and found nothing, he needs to let it go.

"Sebastian, please. You know I would never do something like that. But no, I wasn't here when she went missing. She texted me to tell me she was coming, and she didn't want to even see my face. So, I left."

He huffed out a sigh of relief. "I'm sorry B. I just want to know what happened."

I quickly paced over and embraced him as he let out a sob and wrapped his arms around me for comfort. The other boys, uncomfortable by the sudden display of emotion, quickly began to scatter and find wood for the campfire. By the time they returned, Sebastian and I had set up all of the tents and were getting ready to head out hunting.

The boys quickly got dressed, got their hunting gear ready, had a beer for courage, and were ready to go. They were almost buzzing with excitement at this point as they had only been hunting in areas close to town, never the forests out here. We started our descent down in the valley before I noticed I'd left my arrows back at the camp.

"Go ahead, guys, I forgot my arrows."

"Ahh Bianca, this is why you need to hunt with guns, like the big boys." Jack jokes with me while motioning at his gun. "You sure you're good?"

"Guys, I have hunted out here for years. I'm good." I say while turning to head back uphill. "I'll find you, trust me."

The truth is, I really did need to go back and get my arrows, but it wasn't because I was forgetful. I'd left them there for a reason. I swing past the camp, grab my arrows, and keep heading upward. I needed this advantage to hunt.

It was fairly light still, so I could see them walking down the slopes chatting amongst one another. Then, I spot my prey about fifteen meters back from them. I reach behind me, grab my arrow, set it up, and shoot. The thud I hear when Sebastian's body hits the ground is absolutely priceless.

The other boys hear this too and immediately spin around. When they see him down, they run over to him.

"Silly boys." I whisper to myself with a grin.

"They start to yell and panic as Sebastian's lifeless body is sprawled across the pine needles. I can't stop smiling at this point. I finally feel like I've got them where I want them. I become lost in my thoughts for a moment as I remember how this plan started. They approached me after her funeral, tissues in hand, tears in their eyes, begging for my forgiveness.

I knew that only had remorse for Tegan, not for me. They just wanted to feel better about themselves. I come back to reality as I watch them all panic and start devising a plan. Little do they know I can still hear them from here.

"We have to go back for Bianca, she went back to the tents!"

"Bianca can fend for herself, she's an experienced hunter, trust me!"

"We need to get out of here before we end up like Sebastian!"

All good thoughts boys, but I like the third option, run. Luckily for me, their flight response kicks in, and they leave poor Sebastian's lifeless body behind as they run from me, like I once ran from them; terrified.

I can basically hear their hearts beating out their chests at this point. They are absolutely terrified to meet the same fate as Sebastian. I follow them along the ridge. The height from here meant that I had the advantage no matter where they went.

Up ahead, down from me, I see them crouched under a tree with their backs towards me. I can see Jack clearly trembling at this point. I would be lying if I didn't say that it felt amazing. I once again reach behind me, set up my arrow, and shoot. Caleb turns to notice that Jack has a massive arrow protruding through his body and lets out an audible scream while Jamie sits in complete shock.

If I don't kill Jamie next, the shock will. Without a second to spare, I take out Jamie too. Caleb bullied me the worst at school, so it only makes sense to torture him and kill him last. Like the gutless coward he is, Caleb runs while leaving his friends to die.

Much to my surprise, he heads up the hill this time. In shock, he leaves his gun behind. He must be heading back to the camp, but he won't get far without a gun. This was my time to finish everything. Knowing he was unarmed made it that much better. I run back to the camp and prepare for 'the final scene' as I like to call it. It will take Caleb at least 15 minutes to get back up here, so I begin to prepare.

I start ruining the campsite. I throw, kick, and dirty everything in sight to make it seem like someone else destroyed it. Now, the hardest part. I take out my hunting knife and create a deep wound in my arm. I wince as the blood poured out, but this was a small price to pay for the victory I would soon feel.

Before I hide in the tent and get ready for Caleb to arrive, I hide the car keys to ensure that a quick escape isn't on the agenda. After what feels like forever, I hear hesitant footsteps wander into the campsite.

I begin sniffling and pretending to cry as I hear Caleb walk over. As his footsteps approach, I cry out. "Please, no! Please don't hurt me, please!". I'm shocked by how good my acting is at this point. When the flap to the tent opens and I see Caleb, I jump up and run out to him to hug him and sob.

He looks down at my arm as a mix of sadness and fright flashes across his face. The fear in his eyes is priceless. I bury my head back in his shoulder, so he doesn't see my smile. He asks me what happened, and I spin a tale of how a man came into the campsite as I was trying to find my arrows and attacked me.

"Where are the boys?" I ask him sadly.

"Bianca, he got them. That man. He shot them all. Sebastian, Jack, and Jamie. They're gone. I'm so sorry." He breathes out, clearly exhausted from his walk up the incline.

He brings me in for another hug. As he lets go, I see his eyes wander across to my quiver, where my arrows are kept. At this point, I know he sees the arrows missing, as I only had six to start with. I see a mix of confusion, anger, and shock cross his face as a look of sheer excitement crosses mine.

"Bianca..." he reaches for his gun, forgetting he left it down the incline when he was trying to rush back.

I cut him off immediately, "So, are you going to run? I'll give you a head start."

Without even a second going by, he takes off again. I count to 20 before I chase after him, bow in hand. Within only a few minutes, I catch up and find him with his hands up in surrender and back towards a cliff ledge.

"Bianca, I'm sorry. I'm sorry for hurting you, for bullying you. For everything."

At this point, I raise my loaded bow up towards him. The more he begged and pleaded, the angrier I got.

"So, funny story, I actually hatched this plan the night I killed Tegan."

This confession makes his entire face drop. I could see the betrayal on his face. I revel in it for a few seconds.

"I knew once I killed her, you would all finally want something to do with me. So, when you all preached your forgiveness to me, I accepted. I had you right where I wanted you. Say hi to Tegan for me."

ABOUT THE AUTHOR

Nikita Hillier

Nikita Hillier is a highly educated professional writer based in Western Australia.

She launched her full-time professional writing career back in 2018 after writing as a hobby and part-time for many years beforehand. She has a strong interest in the mental health, thriller, philosophy, pet, and lifestyle niches.

Nikita works for clients globally to create content that is unique, well-researched, and fuelled by passion. She is the ghostwriter behind several best-selling books and can't wait to publish her own books once they are finished. She is currently working on three different books and hopes to publish them in the coming years.

When Nikita isn't writing, she spends her time studying and gaining more knowledge. You can keep up to date with Nikita via the links below!

Website: https://www.nikitahillierwriter.com

Instagram: https://www.instagram.com/nikitahillierwriter/

Facebook: https://www.facebook.com/nikitahillierwriter

LinkedIn: https://www.linkedin.com/in/nikita-hillier-a66495226/

STORY 4

Falling For My Best Friend

I am falling in love with my best friend Sally; she is always there for me when no one else is.

I met Sally after I had a near death experience in a car accident. She was there for me after my accident and she has become my nearest and dearest friend.

I was five years old when I was in a car accident and as I was not wearing a seat belt I went through the front window but luckily at a slower speed so was injured but alive. I had a concussion at the time and that was when Sally met me in the hospital as a young girl but she was so nice and caring.

It took me a while to get where I am now; I have severe anxiety and usually don't want to leave the house. My friends have come and gone over the years but Sally was the only one who was ever there for me, in fact when we spent time with my friends Sally was so quiet that no one even noticed her apart from me.

She strokes my hair in the most reassuring way when I am sleeping and she tells me that I matter, that my life matters and she keeps me strong. She encourages me to look after myself, to go to my gym again and to take my vitamins.

She encourages me to make my hair dressing appointments because being a young woman I love getting my hair done and she reminds me of that. She has encouraged me to make choices for myself to improve my quality of life and encouraged me to complete my nursing degree which I finish this month.

13th June 2022

I'm feeling fit and healthy and I couldn't have made it this far in my life without her. I don't have many friends and family in my life these days and she is all I have in my life and I am grateful for that. I have suffered from severe anxiety and depression all of my life and all throughout my life Sally has been the only constant in my life.

I lost most of my friends when I tried to arrange a meeting in which they would get to meet the person most important in my life. In hindsight I realize now how jealous they were that I had found someone who loves me and that they may not have had that.

They were extremely rude to Sally, walking past her and not acknowledging her or even looking at her. When I told them that Sally was standing right next to them and was trying to get their attention they simply laughed at me and told me that she wasn't real and that I was crazy. I had stopped talking to them after that, because she was real to me and they had insulted us both with their rudeness.

26th June 2022

I feel conflicted, I just learnt that a few former friends have died in bizarre circumstances. We had a horrible falling out, they had insulted me and hurt me when they told me I was crazy and sick in the head. I am still processing these deaths, it feels like I am cursed and though these friends weren't really friends at all it still hurts that we parted on bad terms, permanently.

I've had two former friends pass away between my last journal entry barely within a week. I need to write it as a way to process it because these deaths almost seem suspicious and very strange. I used to be best friends with some of these people, they were too cautious for freak accidents and too proud for suicide.

My former friend, Matt, told me I was so crazy that I must be drinking bleach and at the time that had really hurt. The strange thing was that exactly a few days later Matt had reportedly died by drinking an entire tub of bleach straight from a bottle. The Matt I knew would have never ended it all. When I told Sally she told me that he may have been trying to purify himself to be a better person.

Another former friend, Jane, told me that I would be perfectly matched for a crazy person because I am crazy myself. Jane has been institutionalized and no one knows what happened to her.

Jane had been thirty two when she was institutionalized, a husband and a young daughter who she has now lost custody of. The scary thing is no one knows what happened to her or why she has been institutionalized.

Sally seems to have a huge plan for me but she doesn't want to tell me what that plan is, I trust her a great deal and she has been the only person in my life who I have been able to trust with every fiber of my being.

8th August 2022

I've lost two more former friends in strange circumstances. These two friends were work mates and I went to get drinks with them on Friday night with Sally. I tried to introduce them to Sally as my partner but they acted as if they couldn't see her and laughed at Sally, making rude jokes about appearance.

Samantha died by pressing her face into a waffle machine and then drowning herself in a boiling hot water. I can't comprehend why she would even do that but the investigators on the scene found no sign of a struggle and agreed her death was suspicious.

Sarah died by filling a bath tub up with kerosene, adding turpentine and other poisons and setting herself alight as she took a bath. Investigators ruled the death out as a bizarre suicide but Sarah told me once that she had a bizarre fear of fire.

They were both really promising nurses and I don't know why they were so rude to Sally after I told them she was my partner but they didn't deserve to die and I am shattered. I have spoken to Sally about it and she has only just shrugged and seemed nonchalant about it all.

8th October 2022

Sally is angry at me and I don't know what to do. She caught me researching the death of my former friends and she was not happy. She told me that living in the past was bad for my mental health and that I had to listen to her, she told me that she knew the best and that everything else was a lie.

To make that worse she gave me a cup of cocoa that made me feel very unwell, it had something in it but she had told me at the time it would make me feel better.

I haven't been feeling well lately, at all. Sally tells me that this is all a part of the plan and that my rest right now is crucial to the plan she has which she won't tell me anything about.

Sally tells me she would never hurt me, and to trust her. The problem is that she is starting to get too controlling and it's starting to scare me.

12th October 2022

Part of me is suspicious and I am bed ridden and I caught her tampering with my anti-anxiety medication. She has been taking out the medication from my tablets and throwing them in the bin, she does this every few days so I feel sick and end up needing to rest and vomit. I ask her not to, I beg her to stop throwing my medication out because when I miss a dose I feel my health take a turn for a worse.

Sally has confiscated my phone and my laptop, she has effectively cut off my communication to the rest of the world and though I have always been a hermit I am a bit afraid for my life now. I live alone, and Sally usually visits me, she is the only person who visits me and since I have been sick she has been at my side every day.

I have been pleading with Sally to allow her to give me my medication so I start feeling better and I have begged her to let me near my phone again because otherwise all I do is sleep. I want to get outside and move, I want to leave the house and find help, this doesn't feel right and something is wrong.

I have been bed ridden and too dizzy to move in my dark bedroom with the curtains always being drawn and I no longer have a concept of night or day and as I have no access to my laptop or television I don't know what is happening around me. I don't even know the time of the day, what day of the week it is, all I know is that I am lying in my bed and sweating profusely.

15th October 2022

Sally tells me she is looking after me and nursing me to health but I had been fine right until she had caught me researching the events leading to the death of my friends.

I can't help but to wonder whether she had given me that drink of hot cocoa with something in it to make me unwell and was now withdrawing my medication and communications as a form of abuse and control. She has never told me what her plan for me is and I am starting to feel very concerned for my life and have accepted Sally must have caused the misfortune of my friends.

I want to believe that Sally is punishing me because she loves me and because she doesn't want me to get sick because of her but I am starting to feel afraid of her. Sometimes when I wake up from her she is sitting over me and she is staring straight at my face when I wake up, she watches me sleep but she watches me fall asleep too, and then she is still there when I awake and she hasn't moved.

When I sleep I dream of her taking over me and draining my life force and I don't know whether it's my subconscious warning me of her or something more sinister.

I cannot see my reflection but I haven't eaten a proper meal in days and I am starving but Sally is not bringing me food, she tells me she is unable to bring me food because she finally wants me to understand that she is not real. I don't know what she means by that.

"I'm your imaginary friend, I tried to claim your life in the car crash but you survived and I wanted your soul but figured I'd toy with you because I have all the time in the world. You don't. I want your body and your nursing degree. I want to torment all of the lost souls in the hospitals; you were perfect for my plan."

Her words were so cold and callous and I realized it now, she was never real to anyone but me. She had done real damage because she was a demonic force who had attached to me because of the near death experience I had.

She was never real to anyone I had met but the damage she had done to them was very much real. I knew it now, I had been alone all this time.

ABOUT THE AUTHOR

Natasha Godfrey

Natasha Godfrey is an Australian scare actor, support worker and horror enthusiast who stumbled into the writing world after tumbling down the freelance writing rabbit hole.

Natasha has overcome personal demons to write and publish books on Amazon including Recovering From Self Harm -By a Recovering Self Harmer and Burn that Trauma Bond and as a horror enthusiast is obsessed with horror.

Natasha has also worked with Endless Ink Publishing House and has completed online work through the platform Upwork which was the platform she used to commence her freelance journey.

Writing aside, Natasha is a crazy cat lady, coffee junkie and creative weirdo.

STORY 5

The Elevator

As I was coming to, all I could hear was a man screaming his lungs out. Trying to open my eyes as I felt like my head was physically spinning, I saw the source of the scream.

The man crushed by the unattached seats screamed for only a few moments more and slowly, his voice died out. Time didn't exist for me at that moment; so, I don't know how much it took for me to fight the nausea and get up from my seat, but I was able to, at some point. I walked towards the opening in the plane, thick metal crushed like tin foil, and half of the plane missing.

I walked in the darkness, not looking around me. I saw the dark shapes of people sitting in their seats, but I never looked directly at them but only to the man who was half on the metal floor of the plane and half on the sand.

He must've bled out rather quickly. I wasn't out for long.

With that in mind, I took the few more steps downslope needed to get on the sand from the slanted plane. The orange color screamed at me from the outside seen between the crushed metal and crouching down, I got out of the plane from an opening created by the impact.

The sun out, the bright morning welcomed me to the endless sea that was the desert surrounding my every direction. I didn't know where I was, not even a clue. I didn't know which direction led to civilization, and I didn't know how long I had to survive under this scorching sun and touching the burning sand. Panic clawed at my chest from the inside, trying to get out. Containing it made it feel awful. The thought of going back into the plane made it even worse.

I wasted most of that day looking for anything in the plane. Everyone was dead, and as I looked for any communication device still functioning, I tried my best to not think about my survival, both from the crash and from the days that would follow.

Nothing survived in the plane. Not a single person, not a single electronic device. Taking all the food and water I could get my hands on, I waited for the day, shivering from the cold of the night.

The thought of the plane is ever-present in my head now. The ominous wind whistling through the sands became a calling to me. They call me to my sandy grave. I can't stop thinking about how many people died in this desert, and their bodies would never be found. It's been 3 days since I started walking. I am out of water and food. I left my backpack on the sand in a small dune hours ago, as I no longer needed it.

Every single thought attached to that awful feeling of inner dread vanished as I laid eyes on something shiny in the distance. With legs aching and skin scorched and red from the unrelenting rays of deadly sunlight, I never knew I had the energy in me to run, but I did. I ran towards that shiny something in the distance, and I was right beside it a minute later.

It was an elevator. Stood in the middle of nothing, in a relatively flat spot in the desert, attached to the ground. I had no thoughts as I looked at the metal rectangle but a thought about how much cooler it must be inside. My body was weak, weakened even more from my run towards the elevator. I took one more step forward towards the elevator and collapsed to the ground.

With sand in my mouth and nose, I rose from the sand as dust flew all around me. My eyes wide open and mouth agape, I only woken up from a dream where I was being crushed by the elevator falling on me.

I managed to get myself on my feet and walked the last few steps needed to get into the elevator that was still standing tall in front of me. It was now night, but the bright metal was shining with moonlight, nonetheless.

I wouldn't get to find out if it was cooler in the elevator since the night was freezing cold now, and all I could do was clutch myself with my own hands and bare through the cold as I would do in the previous nights, while looking around the elevator.

It was dark inside the elevator; so, I could only see a slight silhouette in the big mirror attached to the wall of the elevator. Even from this reflection, I knew I looked like a ghost, barely able to stand up, with eyes open wide, body and face unnaturally emaciated.

Looking at the reflection with more detail, I slowly got closer to the mirror and without blinking, my head filled with confusion and that gnawing dread again. I was slowly recognizing the extraordinary situation I was in, and as the realization that I was standing in an elevator in the middle of the desert washed over me, I instinctually escaped my gaze from the mirror and walked towards the control panel of the elevator.

Two buttons. One arrow up, one arrow down. I pressed up without thinking about it, and the dark elevator's sliding door closed, leaving me in total darkness. Then, it moved.

Up?

The slight shake as the elevator started was enough of an indication of my weak nature, so I let my body slowly fall to the ground and with my back touching the cold metal of the walls, I waited as the elevator moved and gravity tried ever so slightly to pull me down.

The ride took a long time. I didn't know how long. Even though I felt it move up, the freestanding elevator had no cable attached above it, or nothing of similar nature. I made myself believe that I was going down, and the arrow pointing up was used to go back up to the surface from where I was heading.

It was impossible to tell now as the elevator moved at a steady place, it might as well have been stationary, and I would almost not realize.

An underground facility? Maybe a depot, a storage of some sort waited for me down there. Even if nobody was there, there would be water. And water, water I needed. I didn't know how long I had before my body fell to the lack of nutrition and water, but it wasn't that long.

In complete darkness, my breathing started becoming faster as I slowly lost the battle of trying to convince myself that the elevator was going down.

It was going up; I knew it deep down. How was it going up? Was the elevator levitating in midair now, with a thin sheet of metal under my feet keeping me from falling hundreds of meters down? The thought didn't help my breathing, or the feeling of dread eating me inside out like a parasite.

As the elevator shook, I held my breath, feeling as ready as much as one could for death as the floor I was sitting on felt like tin foil. I waited, and rather than falling to my death, I saw dim blue lights come and fill the elevator as the door slid open.

I reluctantly got up on my feet. My eyes, slowly getting accustomed to the light, couldn't see what was beyond the door, but I walked through it anyway. I had no choice but to move forward, wherever the desert was now, up or down, only death waited for me back there.

The room I found myself in was colossal. The ceiling's height changed all throughout the room due to stacked pipes the same dark grey color as the ceiling moved around above me. I could see that in some places, the pipes were low enough that I would need to crawl underneath them, and in other places, the ceiling was tens of meters above me.

Everything was painted with a tinge of blue due to the dim lights emanating from the walls. I could see flora all around the room, vines, bushes, batches of mushrooms, and all kinds of weed making their way through the walls and the floor, as well as between the pipes.

Cast with the cold blue like the rest of this place, I slowly walked towards a direction. Because of the intense size of the room, it didn't feel like a particular location mattered. I only chose the direction I walked because the pipes did not lay as low there, that was it.

There was no furniture, no trash, no dirt, nothing but the cold grey metal surrounding me. The only sound was my footsteps bouncing all around this colossal place. Even if I saw a wall to the left of me, the other walls were beyond my sight.

I walked, looking at the ground, trying to decipher if I could see walls ahead of me, looking at the ceiling.

Looking at the ceiling.

Black pipes were jumbled up like a ball of yarn, hanging with a few threads of cable from the pipes, I followed the few cables that managed to escape the ball of chaos and hang down towards me.

I saw something hung from one of the cables. It was around 5 meters above me. Its skin sludge-like, and head bloated like a blowfish, the sight of what I was seeing did not register to my mind for a few seconds.

Its lower body was on the ground, ahead of me, almost hidden beneath a few metal plates. I looked at the mass, getting closer to see it more clearly. Both the upper torso and lower torso were a tinge of bright blue, almost cyan.

I walked closer, and closer. I was now only a few more step away from it. The remainder of the body hanging from the ceiling was now behind me.

The cyan color of the slimy mass called to me to take those last steps forward, and as I did, my body convulsed and almost gave out.

The mass was semi-translucent, with white masses pulsating and traversing inside the slimy mass, as if trying to leave it. The legs spazzed with mystifying motions as in rigor mortis.

With this sight, I pushed myself back almost as an involuntary response to get away from the mass as quickly as possible, and as I realized that the rest of the body was now above me as I took those steps back, I started running in a direction in panic. Which direction, I didn't know. Only thing I wanted to do was to get away from that thing.

My legs about to give out, I saw light coming from a distance, a light most inviting, and familiar. It only took seconds to make my way there, and as I saw the opening to the bright blue sky, I stopped at my tracks. My legs gave out and I fell towards the edge of the hole. My vision blurry and a dark translucent curtain over it, I grabbed the edge of the tear that was both in the floor and the wall and dragged myself forward. Looking down, I saw the desert below me.

So, this is where the plane hit.

Sounds akin to wet meat being squished screamed behind me, and I used my last strength to look back. I saw them, most of them torn up, oozing a white liquid from what could be described as scars on their pulsating cyan bodies. Their top-heavy heads wobbled slightly as they walked towards me. They would tower over me even if I was able to stand up.

I tried to pull myself towards the emptiness ahead of me, and the moment I thought I was able to free myself towards open air, one of them managed to grab my leg, its thin fingers wrapping circles around my leg. I tried as I could, but my grasp on the edge of the hole was only desperate. I screamed towards the open air, hoping for anything human to hear me.

My screams died out as they dragged me farther and farther from the light, now only a speck, and cyan darkness consumed me, only filled with the sounds of convulsing.

ABOUT THE AUTHOR

Umut Ceylan

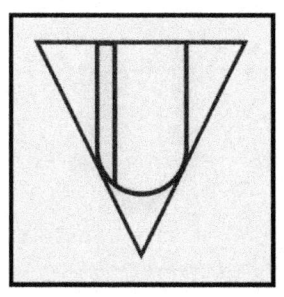

I always look forward to reading, watching, or doing anything with any type of media involving horror and the unknown. From the very tempting and almost glamorous portrayals of the underworld from the start of cinema, from how much we didn't know in the past, and how much we will know in the future, everything can be span into something terrifying to anyone. Being scared, enticed by such visions from the comfort of your couch can be almost cozy, comforting even.

I strive to write about the mysterious of many. My role models in horror include but are not limited to H.P. Lovecraft, Junji Ito, Zdzisław Beksiński, and countless other talents all over the world doing something new and terrifying but enticing and beautiful in their own twisted way at the same time.

I've been writing horror since 2010, starting with Turkish at first, I transitioned into writing in English to reach a wider audience. My goal is to entertain, and invite new worlds into our psyche, thought experiments that scratch that itch at the back of our minds.

See you there.

Other short stories:
https://medium.com/@umutceylan

You can reach me at:
umuthceylan@gmail.com

STORY 6

Shells

Greg dove head-first into the mud-filled trench, a barrage of 50-cal shells following in his wake. He hit the shallow bottom and quickly crawled to one side of the trench, brushing aside the pain from the impact.

He hunkered down, listening intently to the loud clatter of bullets, and tried to figure out the shooter's location. HMG bullets streaking through the morning fog lit up the sky above him. And for the billionth time, Greg wondered why the fuck he had enlisted.

Interestingly enough, Greg knew the reason for his joining the army – and man did he hate it. Three years before the invasion, Greg was a freelance programmer who spent most of his days searching the web for new gigs and trolling people on the internet.

When he wasn't working, Greg was an avid gamer. In fact, his go-to videogames were – you guessed it – First Person Shooter games. One night, furiously high on adrenaline, his dick throbbing from the excitement of a high-octane rampage on his PC, Greg concluded that actual warfare would definitely prove much more exciting. A year later, he was sharing combat rations in a dug-out with several other conscripts.

Fast forward to today; Greg's squad had been tasked to go into the wheat fields east of Bakhmut and collect the bodies of their fallen comrades. Apparently, their commanders had negotiated a so-called 'green area' around the volatile region and the Russians had seemingly complied up until the soldiers' boots touched the blood-soaked soils of the disputed town.

"I bet you a week's MRE's the Russians blow us up the moment we drive into the wheat fields", Greg said to Victor, their six-foot tall sniper, as their truck rumbled down a dirt track toward the yellow fields.

"It's not the Russians you should be worried about Gregori", replied Victor.

"What do you mean 'not the Russians'?"

"You think the Russians just let us into their front yard out of the sheer benevolence of their hearts?" Pauli, the oldest conscript on the team, offered quizzically.

"Tell him, Pauli." Victor urged, his left hand tightening over the green strap of the bolt-action Barrett Model 98B sniper rifle slung over his shoulder. His right hand gripping the metal bar over his head to steady himself, he stared spitefully at Greg, whose crimson face was tinged with uncertainty.

Pauli, his eyes scouring Greg's face for the slightest signs of skepticism, drew in a deep contemplative breath, effectively shooting the suspense in the troop carrier through the roof, and then began his narration.

"Ever since the annexation of Crimea in the south, the commanders on both sides draw straws at a random time each year. The loser essentially offers up the worst of their conscripts for some twisted game of survival. A bloody sacrifice to Dragunov, the Slavic god of modern warfare."

As Pauli went on with his scary story, Greg's face took on a cynical look that slowly morphed into 'mildly amused', and ultimately settled on 'utterly doubtful'.

"Slavic god of modern warfare?" Greg asked skeptically. "Come on man. That the best you got?"

"You heard him man. Look around. We're the fucking sacrifice", answered a short man seated next to Victor. His tiny pale face riddled with anxiety.

"What the fuck do you mean 'Sacrifice'? Man, we could fuck out of here if we wanted to. Even if it were true, nobody drives themselves to their fucking death", Greg retorted suggestively.

"Look up dude. See the drones? Yeah? The slightest deviation from the dirt path and we'll be the 'dead comrades'", Victor replied, his face smiling hard, trying desperately to mask the fear and despair lurking behind his eyes.

Greg looked up at the Bayraktar TB2 drone boldly trailing them in the sky; undaunted, menacing, malignant. And the realization slowly sunk in. This wasn't some sick joke his friends were playing on him, it was real, all of it. His mind painfully grasped the implications of what he had just heard; up until that moment, his life had held no real meaning.

He had been a miserable nobody ever since his birth and here he was, doomed to die an ugly, meaningless death. And as his mind wrapped itself around the concept – his feeble hopes and dreams, the desires for glory on the battlefield, his perverted, twisted desire for gore – all of them slowly flitted into the chilly morning. Jumping ship while they still had the chance, leaving him to die; sad, empty, alone.

"That's not the worst part…" Pauli, having seen the change in

Greg's eyes, went on.

"Both sides have full access to real-time drone footage. And the body cams?" Pauli said, left hand tapping the camera attached to his bulletproof vest, "Live, Hi-Res footage. Twisted fucking rich folks paying some good money to see that dejected look on your face right now."

Greg felt a hot streak of anger rise from deep inside his stomach, creeping up through his skin and neck and wrapping his head and eyes in its fiery grip. In a second, he jumped to his feet and threw his form towards Victor, his eyes staring mad at the body cam turned in his direction.

All the while, his hateful, primal gaze seemed to focus deeper, much, much deeper; beyond the plastic and the lenses, and past the 72-inch, 4K televisions. It stared right back at the malicious, laughing eyes of the rich, overbearing snobs who had fucked him over.

But as he lunged toward Victor, his hands never reached the bodycam. In a moment of utter madness, everyone in the back of the troop transport was tossed into the air like Barbie dolls in a playdate gone wrong as the truck ran over a mine.

****

Greg was violently jolted from his musings when a massive shadow suddenly dropped into the trench behind him. He turned around, eyes clamped shut, hastily brushing aside the heavy machine gun fire that had not-so-long ago held-fast his attention.

Then, pointing the Kalashnikov's muzzle in the general direction of his new-found greatest horror, he pulled the trigger. As if on cue, the HMG fire abruptly stopped, the sinister echo of bullets slowly fading off into the morning. Greg hadn't felt the familiar stubborn recoil of his rifle two seconds ago when he was pulling the trigger for dear life, and as the thunderous silence settled about him, he became ever aware of a persistent "Click!", each time his finger pulled on the trigger.

Slowly opening his eyes, Greg felt a flustered warmth fill his face and cheeks as Victor's bulging form slowly came into focus. His eyes wide with laughter. A nasty grin on his rugged face.

"Friendly fire much?" he asked. Greg, still reeling from the amateur show of fear and incompetence, ignored his squad-mate's snide remark.

"You see any sign of the attackers?" he asked, deft hands swiftly reloading his gun in an apparent effort to save face.

"No. I was tossed into a shell crater the moment we hit the mine. How about you?". Greg held up a hand to his left ear and covered it for a second,

"Fucking tinnitus. I staggered into the undergrowth before it all registered and dove into the ground, quite fucking literally, the moment I heard the burst of HMG fire", he said, gesturing around the trench with his hands and eyes,

"I think about five hundred yards west of us, How about the rest of the squad?"

"The white-faced kid, Fyodor? He's huddled in the bushes next to the busted troop transport. He's got a piece of truck sticking out of his side man, not gonna last very long."

"Fuck! How about Pauli?"

"Pauli is dead, along with the driver, and that other guy"

"Aaah Shit!", Greg said, his face turning ashen as he weighed the odds of their survival in his head. Then suddenly he turned toward Victor with a curious look in his eyes.

"Other guy? What do you mean '…that other guy'. There were five of us, what other guy?"

"I saw three dead guys when I was pulling Fyodor into the bushes"

"You didn't check?"

"Check!? Fucking che… Did you not hear the blasted 50-cal bullets flying all over the place?"

Greg looked at Victor for a moment, his mind processing the gnarly death of two (or maybe three) of his squad and the slow, inevitable death of a fourth. There seemed something strange about him. His eyes maybe? They looked the same; deep-set, brooding, and forlorn. His pale features? No, Victor was your average Slav, snow is probably his default setting, Greg thought. Then he found it.

"What the Fuck man, where's your Bolt-action?". A shadow snuck behind Victor's eyes for an instant, barely noticeable, then an uneasy grin broke to the surface across his face.

"Fucking amateur hour. Must've dropped it when I pulled the punctured kid to cover."

Seeing a chink in the armor, Greg eagerly gobbled up the chance to show-up his long-time tormentor.

"I'll cover you while you make a run for the busted truck. Once you get there, find a weapon, send a signal, and lay down fire while I rush toward you. Clear?"

"Clear!" Victor replied, his knees bent, ready to sprint out of the trench.

Greg moved toward the western side of the trench and pointed his rifle over the top.

"Alright here goes. Three! Two! …"

Greg pulled the trigger and grinned as the Kalashnikov rebelliously lurched in his hands, leaping to life as shells flew out of its muzzle. Victor on the other hand jumped out of the trench and tore toward the mangled troop transport.

Cartridge casings rained down around Greg as he emptied the magazine into the fray. And when the click of the hammer reverberated down to his ears, he drew back his gun and reloaded it, doing it slower this time round, as there was no party to impress.

Mere seconds later, Greg was making a mad dash toward Victor and the welcome cover of the wrecked truck. Why the fuck is nobody returning fire? Greg thought, as he dropped down behind the truck, desperate to catch his breath.

"Damn! Fucking Russians!" Greg swore in between harried breaths.

"I know right?" Came Victor's reply.

Greg's pulse gradually slowed to an even pace. His eyes looking around, getting a feel of his surroundings, glanced over at Victor. At where he thought he'd heard Victor's voice – and then there it was, Victor's bolt-action Barrett Model 98B, with its skeletonized buttstock and fluted, medium-heavy, 27-inch barrel. Lying on the ground next to the broken bodies of the driver, Pauli and... It couldn't be! Then his eyes grew wide. The blood drained from his face and his fraught heart took another dive. Confusion muddled with denial swept across his ashen features, contorting them as it went, and gave him a look of utter incredulity.

Greg stared unbelieving at the torn mess that was Victor's corpse. At the gaping hole on top of his slouched head. At the dogged metal rod that stemmed unnaturally from deep inside his torso, piercing through his clavicle in an obscure and bloody display of torturous finality.

"What... in the ... Fuuuck? NO! Nope! Uh Uhh, Fuck this shit!"

Greg staggered backwards, his head shaking in denial. A cold chill grazed the back of his neck, and then slowly traced the length of his body. He tasted its murky, despondent scent at the back of his throat and felt its sickening, repugnance weigh heavily on his stomach.

He lurched toward the undergrowth as a wave of nausea swept over him, his mind unresponsive to the danger that had all this time driven his attempts at fight and flight, and doubled over, letting out his morning ration of bread and pork.

"Ug... Ugly... shi... shit huh?"

Greg slowly turned his head toward the voice. He was fairly certain he was going mad up until he saw Fyodor's paling face and the god-awful chunk of metal sticking out of his side. He stared for a moment, unsure.

Like a man lost in the desert stares at an oasis; both not so eager to trust their eyes lest the image be a farce. He inched his way toward

Fyodor's fading form, and crouching next to him, felt for a pulse.

"Prom... mise... not to... to bite". Fyodor's strained voice came to him in a half-whisper. In an unusual show of empathy, Greg slowly gripped Fyodor's bloody hands, stared deep into his eyes, and then with a warm, brotherly fondness, whispered into his ears,

"It's all good. I'm right here man."

Without warning, Fyodor's hands slipped from Greg's gentle grip and grabbed his neck, pulling him towards his pasty face. Greg was as scared as he was shocked.

He hadn't known just how fast Fyodor had moved, but in an instant, his fingers were clawing at the death-like grip of Fyodor's cold hands, his scared eyes staring straight into the mad, wide ones of his half-dead squad mate – though suffice to say he didn't look that half-dead to Greg.

"SAY MY NAME! MORTAL!" Fyodor commanded. His voice, not so wavering now, sounded otherworldly. The insane grip on Greg's neck tightened like a vice. Greg's hands seemingly grew a mind of their own as they suddenly reached down for his Makarov PM side-arm and, just as spontaneously, popped a shell into Fyodor's possessed brains.

Greg rolled over next to the corpse, his heart beating out of his chest, his mouth greedily gulping down chunks of oh-so-precious air. His eyes went to the sky and his spirits fell as he recognized the Bayraktar TB2 drone hovering above him, like a vulture biding its time, waiting for its victim to succumb.

He decided then that if he was going to die, at the very least it would have to be on his terms. He felt the end draw ever closer as he slowly lifted the PM to his head. He looked up at the TB2 and at the single munition held in its tiny bomb rack.

"Suck my balls you miserable bourgeois fucks!" He shouted, grabbing his crotch, in a final insolent gesture of defiance. And pulled the trigger.

A minute later, Greg was still alive, but he couldn't move his head from the massive pain in his temple. He tried moving his arm and felt a searing pain shoot up through his whole side. A fucking squib, he thought to himself.

Greg was an avid gun junkie who cleaned his pistol almost every day without fail. As far as he was concerned, death by firearm malfunction sounded like a bad joke. Then painfully glancing over at Fyodor's corpse, Greg saw a darkness flare up behind the lifeless, mocking eyes. As the life slowly seeped out of him, Greg wasn't afraid; instead, he felt an unfamiliar sadness, a deep despondent sadness.

His gaze strayed skywards toward the ominous drone, and his eyes welled up as the single mortar shell hurtled down toward him.

ABOUT THE AUTHOR

Edwin Onserio

Onserio is a student and ghostwriter from Nairobi, Kenya. He freelances on Upwork and especially enjoys writing Horror fiction, Thrillers, Spicy romances and everything in between.

He's big on Rock music and is a huge fan of Haruki Murakami. Aside from reading books he enjoys collecting old stuff – He was born in 2001 so his idea of 'old stuff' spans anything pre-1999.

He's the proud owner of a Sony Walkman WM-34, and a Saw 2004 VHS Tape.

Contact him on Upwork via the link below:

Upwork freelancer:

https://www.upwork.com/freelancers/~01c1aacf309dceac9e

STORY 7
Convenience Store

"Mom, it's fine. It's just for one night," sighed Layla into her phone.

Collapsing onto the bed of her airport hotel room, she couldn't help but think how it was nothing more than a cramped little cube stuffed with basic amenities. "This is what living in hell must be like," she thought to herself.

"Yeah... they're probably giving out free meals with a voucher or something..." Layla said as she looked out the room's only window, so small it might be a hanged painting. You could just about hear her mom on the other end, going on and on about those damned airlines, their reckless delays, and refund policies.

"No, I don't think they'll give me a refund. Don't worry too much, I'll see you in less than twenty four hours," Layla assured her while she massaged her own temples.

"Alright mom, it's late, I love you, bye!" *Click!*

As she laid there staring at the ceiling, the quietness became unbearable after her chaotic day. Thankfully she couldn't keep her eyes open for long. Layla plugged her phone on the nightstand, and switched the lights off. The only thing you could see then was the view outside her window—a town that was as dogged tired as she was.

It was sprawling industrial compound, everywhere you'd look there'd only be concrete and lifeless tarmac. Why would they bother putting an airport all the way out here? But then again, that's what humans are like. We have a knack for filling every nook and cranny with traces of our small lives.

Like that time scientists sent drones down to the deepest trench in the ocean, only to find plastic waste. Chocolate, candy, and chip wraps, imagine them floating in the darkness, all the way down there where life was alien like. Plastic waste swimming amongst bioluminescent fish, who's to say they didn't have lives of their own?

Laila burst her eyes open, "Chocolate, candy, and chips", she mouthed. In the midst of it all, she realized she'd forgotten to eat. Her last proper meal was on the plane, and that was at least five hours ago. Now, the hunger pangs were impossible to ignore.

"Ughhh…" she reached for her phone, 2.16 am was emblazoned in cold white letters.

Laila wasted no time and dove straight into her maps app, she punched in "nearest convenience store", and scrolled through. Just as she thought, everything was closed. Even her mini bar stood empty. So much for airline hospitality huh? That was just another dead end in a day full of dead ends, and she felt like she'd be dead too if she didn't have something to eat soon.

"Goddammit!" Layla rushed to put her coat on. She slammed the hotel room on her way out, gathering enough adrenaline to keep her sleepiness at bay. The world outside was indeed eerily quiet, anything could jump out at any given moment, but then again, why would anything do that in a place like this?

She walked past a 7-Eleven, confirmed it was indeed closed. Then her maps led her to 'Marche', she assumed it was a mom-and-pops shop. But that was also, very predictably, closed. So Layla found herself aimlessly wandering through narrow alleys made of concrete and steel. She made her way up and down those lanes, sauntering over to every faint hint of a neon sign she could make out in the horizon. Until finally, she saw it in, an oasis in the desert.

At the end of a long particularly narrow alley, Layla saw an open convenience store! A friendly man on a neon sign waved, "Open twenty four hours!". God might just exist after all, and he seems like a forgiving one indeed.

Ding dong! an invisible bell chimed when she pushed the door open. Behind the counter, sat a bespectacled old man solving a crossword puzzle, he looked up at her, and Layla gave him a polite nod. "That guy must be ancient," she thought. The old man didn't pay her much attention though, and went straight back into solving his puzzles.

Layla went poking around the store aisles, but they were mostly empty, which was relatively normal for this hour. She saw boxes of cereal, toilet paper, one off fruits and veggies, but no chocolates, candy, or chips. She couldn't even find those microwaveable meals.

"Umm... excuse me?" Layla asked the man.

"Yeah?"

"You wouldn't happen to have any snacks out back do you?"

The old man raised an eyebrow, "Snacks? You mean like a banana? Think we have one right there."

"No no, I mean... yes a banana's a snack... but I'm looking for something less healthy and more hearty, something filling you know?

Like chocolates, candy, chips? Microwaveable meals?"

The old man leaned back on his chair and crossed his hands in front of him, "Them chocolates aren't always especially filling miss, and eh microwaveable meals huh? Do you have any idea where you are?"

"Um… a convenience store?" now it was Layla's turn to be confused, "Look, if it's not too much trouble, please go back there and check out if you have anything for me? I've had a really long day and I could really use something to eat."

"Miss, this ain't the place to be looking for something microwaveable…" he thought for a bit, "But then again I never tried it myself, maybe some of me customer actually do that with their takeaways."

Layla was certain this guy was trying pull her leg. But then she saw an empty tip jar in front of him, "Oh is that what this is about?" she thought.

"Sir, microwaveable or not, I'm willing to pay whatever it is for those meals, you can triple the price for all I care!"

"You sure? They already cost a fortune," he asked her.

Layla took out four hundred-dollar-bills from her wallet and slammed them in front of him. "You think I was kidding?" said Layla. The old man looked her up and down, "You're a weird one miss, and eh… I guess I could give you a discount, and that'll be enough for a small cut," he pocketed the money, then got up.

"I can serve 'em to you with some mashed potatoes you know, it'll keep you full til morning for sure," he said as he led her to the back door. "Come on now, we'll go get it where it's fresh."

The door opened to a tunnel, a closed-in space with wall-to-wall pipes. Layla glanced at the store's front door one last time before she ducked in after him, hungry little Alice following her hunger that was not-a-so-little rabbit.

The tunnel was colder than she'd expected, Layla shivered and blew into her cupped hands. She kept them cozy in the pocket of her coat, "Jeez, you weren't kidding about keeping 'em fresh huh?" she asked. The Old Man stopped and turned to her, "Huh? Off course! See I only serve the best!" Layla nodded, impressed, and followed him along without another word.

They got to the end of the tunnel and the old man unlocked a heavy steel door, he struggled to push it open, and when he did, Layla saw straight into rows and rows of the beheaded bodies. Men and women hanging from meat hooks.

They came in every race, age, and size you could think off. Most of them were missing more than just their head, a guy there only had one leg, another one only had both hands, a woman was just a hanging torso. Layla stood there with her mouth open, the wind was instantly knocked out of her.

"Well don't just stand there, come on in and pick one!" hollered the Old Man.

"Ermm... yeah... about that..." Layla stepped in and carefully shifted around the hung bodies, "I was thinking... of you know...ummm... other meat?"

"You mean the brain? Four hundred ain't gonna get you a cut of a brain missy! Choose one and I'll give you a prime cut," he pulled the woman's torso in, "She ain't so bad right? A best seller these days."

"Uh-huh…" replied Layla, full of apprehension.

The old man thought for a few second and nodded, "Oh I get it! You're one those folks who can't eat unless they know exactly what they're eatin! Lemme fetch you a folder of who's who so you can get a better look," and just like that, he weaved his way to a corner office space. Layla followed him, still being careful not to touch any of the bodies.

"Let's see umm…." the man stood there with a huge binder folder in hand, he flipped through people's info. Layla took a peek and saw that if he wanted to, he could tell her exactly who they were, what they did, where they lived, and maybe will even indulge her with how they ended up there.

"Umm… that won't be necessary thank you," said Layla, she was shivering from head-to-toe and it wasn't just from the cold.

"Huh?" the Old Man raised his eyebrow at her again, "So what's yer problem eh?"

"Well… it's just that I'm…. new… to this…" she motioned to the bodies, "The folks in the hotel they um… they didn't tell me what to expect."

The Old Man's face instantly lit up, "You shoulda said so missy! First timer eh? I'll choose something special for ya."

He happily waddled over to the torso woman and brought out a large meat cleaver out of nowhere. Layla was on the verge of a panic attack, when he said, "Now you go right along back to the shop alright? I'll get everything done and bring it right over." But Laila just stood there, her eyes darted between the hung bodies, the knife, the Old Man, the limbs, it was all too much!

The Old Man walked over, knife in hand, and... put his hand on her shoulder, "Missy? You wanna eat out here in this cold? Be my guest!" Layla faced him with wide eyes and shook her head. She hurried out the steel door, past the corridor of pipes, and emerged out the shop's back door.

Feeling somewhat safer, she stood there hyperventilating, clutching her chest. Her heart felt like it might jump right out. She saw the exit, the front doors were right there, she could just walk out right now and forget about all this. Except then-

Her stomach growled.

Only then did she remember why she was here in the first place. She remembered the flight, the roaming through the night, the beacon of hope at the end of the dark alley. And most important of all, she remembered she was hungry!

And now she could smell it, the sweet smell of barbecued meat, "Barbecued flesh... human flesh... some woman's breasts?" She thought to herself.

Layla held on tight to the counter and steadied herself. She took a few deep breaths and closed her eyes, "Think... Goddammit, think!" she exclaimed to herself. And when she opened her eyes, it dawned in on her.

She could stay! She could stay... and eat the steak... and no one will ever find out. She was in the middle of nowhere and it seemed like people came here all the time for something like this right? And hell, she already paid four hundred dollars for it, so she might as well.

All this ran through her head when the Old Man came in with a plate of hot sizzling steak, topped with gravy and mashed potato, it looked absolutely appetizing. He pulled over a chair for her and Layla sat down, she stared at her hot-home-cooked-meal.

"Buon appetito! Sorry eh, we usually have tables properly set up out back, but you came in on a slow day and I was just about to close up."

Layla nodded and took a slice out of her steak. She took a bite. And she chewed, and she swallowed, all while the Old Man stood and watched proudly.

"So whaddaya think eh?" he asked her.

Layla looked him dead in the eyes and said, "You know what? It's actually not bad, but I do think I'd prefer a good sirloin."

ABOUT THE AUTHOR

Pia Diamandis

Pia Diamandis, (Jakarta, 1999) is a horror screen and fiction writer who sometimes doubles as an art curator. After finishing her Art History studies in Istituto Marangoni Firenze, she now works as assistant to horror/action film director, TimoTjahjanto - https://mubi.com/cast/timo-tjahjanto

From time to time, she will write film & art columns for online media like Tirto.id - https://tirto.id/author/piadiamandisutm_source=tirtoid&utm_medium=lowauthor and the Gen-Z culture collective, Broadly Specific - https://broadly-specific.com/author/piadiamandis/

She has co-curated an exhibition for Museo Salvatore Ferragamo (2022), performed as assistant curator for the Forme Nel Verde - https://www.formenelverde.com/ outdoor sculpture festival (2018), and worked as a consultant for state museums in Jakarta (2019 - 2021).

While in terms of scary things, she enjoys all things gore and creature horror, particularly those rooted in local lores that are set in current times.

You can find her on instagram @pia_diamandis

Or check out her full portfolio at https://linktr.ee/Pia_diamandis

STORY 8
Omen

Jess gave a shriek in terror as a cockroach crawled on her hand as she drank her morning coffee to prepare for a day at work. She slapped the disgusting slug off her arm and squished it, deciding that the shock had woke her up more effectively than her cup of coffee.

What was frightening was that Jess had been having reoccurring dreams about eating cockroaches for a while and to have one crawl on her arm was too much of a coincidence.

Jess worked as a travel agent and would frequently pass billboards and images and busy traffic on the way to her work. Lately she had noticed a few people who would stop and stare at her but there was nothing friendly or curious about the way these people would stare at her.

She knew their faces from somewhere and there was a strange look of recognition in the way they looked at her. There were four of them, two young children, one young woman and one younger man and they would watch her with a cold expression and would never return her smile.

Jess looked at her watch and locked the door as she walked to work and tried to remember her dreams. Jess was an intuitive type who paid attention to her dreams and what her subconscious was trying to tell her and the fact she was starting to feel stalked in her real life made her paranoid.

She could sense there was something amiss that her dreams were warning her of and she knew it was no coincidence that strange things were happening.

Jess passed a billboard with a yacht on it that read YOU WILL NEVER BE SEEN AGAIN and she couldn't help to shudder at the message. Those were the same words a cruel former partner had used once and the nasty words stayed with her.

Jess knew the message was not intended to be threatening but in her dreams she was being drowned from a yacht by an unforeseen force and it felt too real. Something was off, the advertisement was also from her company so though she knew it was approved by management it felt like an attack.

Her dreams featured yachts, turbulent oceans, eating cockroaches, syringes and being injected by poison and they made no sense to her when she was awake but she knew they carried a hidden warning. Jess passed the four familiar faces, two young adults as they walked hand in hand and offered her a glare.

She shuddered, both of their eyes were slightly bloodshot and she wondered if they were under the influence of something. She would always see them there, doing the same action but different times of the day. No one else seemed to notice them and they only made eye contact with her.

She passed the school; the two children who always stared at her with wide pale eyes were waiting for her by the chain link fence. Jess noticed there were other children playing behind them but not interacting with her or the other children. Jess lowered herself at their level and smiled when the boy spat a cockroach in her face as the girl giggled.

Jess gave a yelp and brushed the cockroach away in disgust, she glared down at the two children to see them both smiling up at her. She decided they were just two cruel children and that the weird couple must have been their parents and left it at that. Jess didn't want to think about it or read into it anymore because it felt too real to her.

Jess arrived at her work, ignoring another billboard depicting a yacht in a turbulent ocean with no real relation to her company this time. Just a random billboard sign of a yacht in a turbulent ocean exactly the same yellow one she kept seeing in her dreams.

She greeted her colleagues and sat in her office and for a moment when she looked into her computer screen she thought she saw a face behind her in her reflection and jumped.

"Relax Jess! Are you alright? You're a little jumpy." Anna was the "mum" of her workplace and sat next to her to offer her some chocolates. "Are you OK?"

"Thank you Anna, I am now. Thank you, I need these." Jess tried to smile, she was only six months into her new job and though she loved it she didn't want her colleagues thinking she was unhinged. Jess looked down at the chocolates in her hand only to see that there was a cockroach crawling on her desk. She got up and shrieked and Anna caught her, holding her.

"Whoa!! Take it easy! Are you up to this today?" Anna blurted out, trying to calm Jess down. "What happened?"

"There was a cockroach crawling on my desk!!!" Jess blurted, she looked frantically for it but she couldn't see it but she knew she wasn't hallucinating.

"Jess, where did it go? Jess, are you feeling OK? You can go home if you want."

Jess broke down, it was bad enough having nightmares, seeing weird people, having kids spit cockroaches in her face and seeing the nightmarish dream like visions in the real world. "I'm sorry, it's just been a bad morning.

I haven't been sleeping too well and these kids spat in my face this morning." Jess blurted, she felt a bit better for being honest with Anna about what was happening but wasn't ready to get to the truth.

"Honey, take the day off. We will pay you for today. Go home and get some rest." Jess focused on Anna's shirt, again, a graphic image of a yacht in a turbulent ocean flashed on Anna's pure white shirt. Jess knew she was losing her sanity by the minute.

Jess gathered her stuff and ignored the stares of her colleagues as she stepped outside to hail a taxi. The taxi driver pulled over and Jess crawled into the back seat. When the taxi driver turned to smile at her for a split second Jess thought she saw the face of a demon on the mans face and gave a shriek of terror.

"Whoa!! Lady!! I'm sorry. I didn't mean to startle you. Where am I driving you?" The taxi driver was kind enough and Jess felt embarrassed by her reactions now, it was just for a second the man didn't look human.

"Shit. I'm sorry. I'm just feeling unwell and had to leave early. I live a few blocks from here, the two story brick house, you can't miss it."

The taxi driver nodded and they drove in silence, Jess went to pay the taxi driver who suddenly spoke up.

"Y'know, I was like you once. I kept seeing things, I just want you to know there is a group chat for people like us. It's a web page called Strange Happenings and I am a moderator. Hang in there, it gets easier I promise."

Jess nodded politely and paid the driver. She had no intention of looking at the web page but took a mental note to check it out once she knew she wasn't going crazy.

Jess made a beeline for her bathroom and decided to apply a face mask, if she was going to take the day off she was going to do something nice for herself. She was patting the mask on her face when to the left of her she noticed the same demon figure standing to her left in her reflection. She dropped her fragrant face mask bowl and it cracked on the floor as Jess shrieked.

That was real, she knew that was real because it was real enough for her to drop the expensive mixture of face mask cream in one of her favorite bowls. Jess looked back up at the mirror to see some strange words scribbled on the mirror with her face cream which now had cockroaches crawling in it.

There was a faint reflection of a yellow yacht in a turbulent ocean behind her in the mirror and Jess felt the room spin as she read the words scrabbled on her mirror in her face cream.

YEVEREE ANBOLIN LEN USAGWI

Jess trembled in shock and fainted when she realized that she was in fact staring at an anagram. She didn't need to translate it to know it read YOU WILL NEVER BE SEEN AGAIN.

Jess blacked out for a few minutes and groggily came to with a throbbing headache, she didn't know if she was concussed or what to look for but felt despite an ear splitting headache that she was OK. In that time she dreamed of being injected with poison and being forced to eat cockroaches and the demon tormenting her was torturing her in her dreams.

Jess switched on her laptop and searched the web page that the taxi driver had recommended for her. It featured first hand reports of the same phenomena that was happening to her and Jess realized now that she was not alone and the driver had been right.

Jess read that the cockroaches symbolized poor self image and eating disorders, Jess had suffered from both of them and this made sense to her. The poisonous injections symbolized being influenced by negative influences in life and Jess had a near death experience only a few years ago.

She read that the demon stalking her and others was attracted to people who had been through trauma because they were still building up psychological walls against their pain. Jess had almost died once at the hands of an abusive partner and back then and in her mind's eye she remembered a bright yellow yacht in a turbulent ocean at the time.

Luckily her housemate at the time had thrown him out and rang the police but the scars of almost being drowned stayed with her.

His words back then had been "you will never be seen again."

The general consensus seemed to be that the demon had almost claimed her that time she thought she was going to die and was disappointed that she survived. She realized that the demon was getting more insistent and intended to literally drive her to insanity so she would take her own life or end up institutionalized. Jess tried not to panic but she knew that she had every right to panic, so she reached out in a new post and introduced herself to see if it was too late for anyone to help her.

There was a knock at the door then and Jess jumped slightly to answer it, it was the cab driver who had helped her earlier. He stood with a soft smile on his face and nodded politely at her.

"May I come inside Jess?" The taxi driver asked politely and Jess nodded and invited him inside.

"How did you know I was in trouble and needed help? Can you help me?" Jess asked softly, she was touched by the man who went to the trouble to come back to check on her after dropping her home.

Jess looked at the man as he fell silent, he had a cruel smile on his face as he gazed at her unblinking and started to eat a cockroach in front of her.

"Jess, you never told me your name." The cab driver smiled and she watched in horror as the man's features morphed into something demonic. "You just invited me in and now you will never be seen again."

ABOUT THE AUTHOR

Natasha Godfrey

Natasha Godfrey is an Australian scare actor, support worker and horror enthusiast who stumbled into the writing world after tumbling down the freelance writing rabbit hole.

Natasha has overcome personal demons to write and publish books on Amazon including Recovering From Self Harm -By a Recovering Self Harmer and Burn that Trauma Bond and as a horror enthusiast is obsessed with horror.

Natasha has also worked with Endless Ink Publishing House and has completed online work through the platform Upwork which was the platform she used to commence her freelance journey.

Writing aside, Natasha is a crazy cat lady, coffee junkie and creative weirdo.

STORY 9
Shower

They always walked away. With a suitcase in one hand and a coat in another, they always chose to walk away.

"Maybe I'll see you around," is what they would say. But a few months together in the wretched, collapsing heap of a boarding house wasn't enough to establish that kind of bond.

They never called, never came back. Who would? Somewhere out there, the women who used to be tenants had managed to pursue their dreams, living in a fancy apartment in a better part of the city. It was easy to forget the shoddy house they had briefly called home.

But no, not her. She couldn't do that. She was, for one, the landlord. Or was it lady, is that what it was called? The latter didn't sound as good to her. Less… powerful.

And she was a strong woman. She was thin, but muscular. Years of tending to an old house would do that to you.

As she watched her oldest tenant wave goodbye, something inside her wanted to scream, "*Take me with you, please!*"

But the words never left her mouth and remained bubbling in her throat. After all, she had no choice.

She sighed and made her way up the winding staircase. Each step creaked as she put her weight upon it. *Creak, creak,* it went, until she reached the last landing. *Creak.*

What was that?

She inhaled deeply and walked straight ahead, towards the corridor. It felt damp and dark.

Drip, drip, went the drops of water as they echoed from the puddle in the communal bathroom.

"The shower's broken again," Edith complained. "And can't we do something about the water?"

"I'll take a look at it."

She said that every week. But every week it was the same. She didn't have much money to upgrade the facilities. If she did, she would have left long ago instead.

She grabbed a glass of water from the tap. She was used to getting water from the bathroom. After all, all the water came from the same place.

The water was discolored and tasted rancid. She could taste the nastiness rise up to her nose. But she swallowed it anyway. Bottled water was too much of a luxury for her.

She set down the glass and leaned over the sink. She thought about the bills she had to pay. Taxes, too. Then there was mom's meds. But she could barely think. The dripping sound of water echoed in her head, making her feel irritated and out of focus.

Deciding to get out of the bathroom, she took a step forward.

"*Cold..*"

She turned around to see her reflection in the mirror. Pale, her eyes wide open with a panicked expression.

"Are you okay?"

"Jesus!"

They both jumped. Edith stared at her.

"Sheesh, calm down. I was just worried because you kinda seemed... out there? Are you okay?"

"Yeah, yeah. I'm good. I just... It's been a long day."

"Yeah, sure. Okay."

Edith was the one who ended the awkward exchange and walked up to the sink.

"Hey, clean up, would you?" Edith called out.

"What? I put the glass back."

"Not that. Your hair. Next time you brush it, can you make sure you don't leave a bunch just hanging in the sink?"

That night she laid on her bed, dazed. This always happens. It began months ago. Strange things that she couldn't explain. She described herself as a pragmatic person, but even the logical excuses in her mind had limits. She shut her eyes.

It was cold and she felt numb. But at the same time, she felt light. Something rippled around her and began to envelop her body.

She opened her eyes and saw... her. She was naked. Her eyes were wide open, stark white. She leaned close, her brown hair floating around both of them. She felt the strands tickle her cheek.

The woman opened her mouth and reached out. She screamed, but no sound escaped her lips.

"Leave me alone!"

She mouthed out the words that were drowned out, as if she was underwater. She flailed her arms around, hoping it would scare the woman away. But they felt heavy.

"No! No!"

She screamed at the top of her lungs, hoping she could somehow free herself from what she was experiencing. Finally, her voice broke through. She felt her throat become hoarse as she screamed louder and louder. Then she heard someone calling her name.

Edith was kneeling in front of her, frantic. Beside her was Sally, another tenant.

"Oh, god. Are you okay? We… We heard you screaming."

"W…why are you in my room…?" She sputtered out. She could taste blood in her mouth. She knew her screaming had wrecked her throat.

"What are you talking about?" Sally asked, raising an eyebrow.

She looked around and shivered. She was cold and wet. And she was sitting in the bathroom, the shower head still dripping with foul water.

She quickly got up, embarrassed.

"Do you need help? Should we go to the doctor?" Edith asked.

"No, no. I don't want to make a big deal out of it. I was sleepwalking, and I slipped, maybe."

"Uh, I don't think sleepwalking involves getting into the shower and screaming at the top of your lungs at 2AM," Sally said.

"I know, I'm sorry."

"Maybe you should get some rest. Go to a bar or go bowling, for a change. Being cooped up in this creepy house is probably stressing you out," Edith suggested.

"No, no. I'm too busy," she lied. In fact, she had lots of time. Only she didn't have the money to play around.

"Well, maybe get some sleep. All of us need it, that's for sure," Sally added. "Good night."

The two of them left, retreating into their rooms. She stood there, clutching the towel wrapped around her body. Maybe Edith was right. It was just the stress. But if so, why could she still feel someone watching her?

It didn't end there.

"Help me, please."

"I'm cold."

"Why did this happen to me?"

Strange voices whispered in her head as she scrubbed the bathroom tiles. What started out as idle thoughts gained a voice and started to whisper in her ears. She tried to ignore it, but she couldn't. If only they at least had something nice to say.

She stood up and stretched. Kneeling on the floor made her dizzy. She shut her eyes and suddenly the woman's face was in front of hers. Only this time, that empty, white stare was gone. Instead, there were only hollow orbs where they had been. Black matter dribbled out of the holes, landing on the floor with a wet splat.

She opened her eyes, gasping for breath. She grabbed the glass and opened the tap. Brown, muddy water overflowed into the glass. She yelped, dropping the glass.

"What happened?" Sally yelled.

"I... I broke the glass."

"Yeah, I can see that. Why?"

"The water. It surprised me."

"You get surprised by water? Wow, I didn't see that coming."

"You don't understand. It was..."

*What?"

Sally stared at her, her arms folded.

"No, it's nothing."

"Sheesh. Get a grip. It's enough that I'm living in this creepy-as-hell haunted house just to get by. Surely I don't have to deal with a cuckoo landlady, right?"

"No, I'm fine. I just... need some rest."

She walked out of the bathroom as soon as she tidied up the broken shards on the floor. She knew that her tenants noticed something different about her. She had always tried to be as reliable as she could. It was her strategy to keep them from moving away. She couldn't bear to stay in the old house alone.

Maybe if she told someone about the things she was seeing... No, nobody would believe her. In fact, it would probably scare them away.

If everyone left, she would be forced to leave. She'll be free, but then what? She didn't finish school, she didn't look attractive, and she didn't have anything to boast about. Who would take her? Where would she work?

If only her mother didn't get sick after stubbornly holding onto their ancestral home, blowing all her savings on renovations that barely made a difference. If only her mother let her finish school, set her free, let her escape from this curse of a home.

But it was impossible. She couldn't make the plunge now. She had to pay for mom's meds, the hospital bill, the nursing home...

She needed a bath. The rank and cold water woke her up. She hoped the scent of cheap shampoo would at least mask the terrible smell.

She had started to calm down when she felt the air grow colder. She shivered. There was a heavy feeling above her.

She continued to scrub hard, rinsing as fast as she could. Suds from her shampoo fell on the tiles, followed by damaged blonde hair from her aggressive scrubbing. Only when she looked down, the hair was brown.

She looked up. Nothing.

"This is stupid."

She stopped. There was a low groan. She looked up again to see a pale hand reaching inside the stall from outside the door. She jumped back, cornering herself to the wall. The hand slowly moved across the door to the wall, moving towards her.

"No, leave me alone! I didn't do anything wrong! Why are you doing this to me?"

"Cold, cold..."

"I can't help you! Leave me alone!"

The hand was inching closer to her now. With a burst of strength, she leapt out of the stall, landing on the floor with a heavy thud.

She rolled over to find two pale legs standing a foot away from her.

"No, get away!"

"Dark. Lonely."

"Help us. Help."

"Friend..."

"No! I can't! I don't…"

She crawled backwards frantically, but the figure in front of her seemed to move in sync with her. Their distance stayed the same.

"Stay away!"

"What's wrong?!"

Edith quickly helped her up, throwing a towel over her.

"I..I..."

"OH MY GOD! What is that?"

Edith was pale as a sheet as she pointed at the figure. She turned her head in time to see the thing vanish into a cloud of smoke.

"What's going on? What's wrong with you two?" Sally asked as she ran into the bathroom. They were both deathly pale.

"What was that?"

It was only her and Edith in the dining room. For some reason, Edith was able to see it. She was glad that she wasn't going crazy, but at the same time, it cemented the fact that what she saw was real.

"For the past few months, I've been seeing things. Hearing voices," she explained. "Visions of someone asking for help. Strange noises. Whispering. Breathing. I thought I was going crazy. But you saw it too. Edith, I... I'm glad I could finally talk to someone about it."

"I...I can't handle this. This is weird! And scary. I... can't stay here anymore."

She felt her heart sink.

"What? Why? Edith... it's nothing. They're harmless. Besides, you're the best friend I have."

"I've been thinking of going anyway. I found a job and a cheap apartment down South. Maybe it's time. And I.. I'm not your friend.

You're just my landlady. It's... sorry."

Edith spoke frantically but was decided. Nothing could change her mind.

Even when she knocked on Edith's door in the middle of the night, nothing changed. Edith simply chose to ignore her. She felt anger in the pit of her stomach. If only the bad things never happened.

"Edith's gone."

Stella announced this over breakfast the following day.

"She left, you know. Must be in a hurry. She forgot most of her stuff. I can take them, right?"

She couldn't respond. Her mind was floating somewhere else.

"Well, guess I'm the last one. But you should look for more tenants soon. I'm thinking of splitting as well soon. Boyfriend offered to split the rent at his place."

"Yeah, you go do that."

She didn't care much about Sally. She was rude and sassy.

And in a week, she was gone.

Now it was truly just her in the house. The floorboards creaked as she walked. Heavy steps. Not just hers, but another, then another. She was not truly alone.

"Cold."

"Lonely."

"...friend."

"I know. I know how it feels."

She slowly climbed up the stairs. Opening the door, she felt the cold evening air on her skin. She walked up to the water tank and opened the hatch. She dipped a finger into the water. It was cold.

She put her foot into the water, then another, and shivered.

"...Out."

"I can't do that. But you don't have to be lonely anymore."

She lay in the cold, rancid water. She closed her eyes, feeling the water slowly envelop her body. She felt something hit her shoulder. She opened her eyes and saw Edith staring at her with eyes wide open.

"We're not your friends."

She ignored the voices. Why can't they say something nice for a change?

She felt her body sink to the bottom of the rancid, murky water.

"Cold. Together."

She smiled. Now that sounded like music to her ears.

ABOUT THE AUTHOR

Lizzette Adele Ardeña

"Addie" is a freelance content writer based in the Philippines. She works on articles and short story assignments after finishing work at her primary workplace. When it comes to writing, she enjoys horror the most.

Since starting freelance writing in 2017, she has delivered short stories, eBooks, and interactive fiction scripts in various genres. Horror and thriller are her most predominant works.

In her free time, she crochets children's clothes while watching horror movies or listening to podcasts about serial killers. Addie loves potatoes and dairy products.

She currently lives with her family, including three dogs and a cat.

Thank you so much for purchasing my book!

If you have the time, it would help me a lot if you could leave a review or just rate my book.

Printed in Great Britain
by Amazon